Sherlock Holmes and the Count Dracula Affair

John Pirillo

"The fire that ignites man's consciousness is not one of the earthly values such as gold, property, power, or control.

The fire that ignites man's consciousness is a kinder quality, of consideration, humility, love, and generosity.

When that fire is quenched, the value of a man's soul becomes besot with the pestilence of greed, lust, anger, and control.

-- Sherlock Holmes

"Fact and truth are not necessarily the same, but effects thereof are not only inevitable but meaningful."

-- Sherlock Holmes

"Help me!" She cried out, backing away from the statuesque redhead that reached for her.

"No one will hear you now."

"Please, don't harm me! Don't harm my baby!"

The mother clasped her child closer to her breast. It was silent.

"My baby!" The mother cried. "Have mercy!"

Mariette smiled into the woman's face. She had her clutched by the throat. "Oh, don't worry about your child. I shall take quite loving care of her."

She glanced at the baby's face, noting the pink bonnet over its head. "But of course, it is... her."

She smiled at the mother. "I'll grant you one wish and one only."

"Anything!"

"You or the baby?"

The mother gave her a surprised look, then slowly knelt, the woman's hand still about her throat, and laid her baby down.

"Wise choice!"

Mariette jerked the woman to her feet and chomped on her beautiful young neck, finding the arteries immediately and pulling on them, like one might soda through a straw.

She sucked the woman's blood through her lush, delicate veins so fast that the woman shrunk and shriveled like a dried prune. She tossed her aside and picked up the baby in the bundle she had snatched from the mother to lure her to the rooftop.

The baby had its eyes open. Staring at her. It let made a cute sound and reached for her nose.

"Maybe I'll keep you," she said in a sweet voice.

The baby giggled and reached again.

She allowed it, but her eyes were on the fallen mother. It had worked. It always worked. Desperate to escape a life they couldn't bear to live any longer, seeking something, anything out of desperation, she had little to do to seduce them into giving up their blood.

And the best part of it was…it made her feel powerful as well as satiated.

For a time.

Mortals were such fools.

Epicurean Delight

"Ahh!" Dorian sighed with pleasure, as the young woman gazed into his eyes, his arms embracing her lovingly, their bodies conjoined as all lovers must at times.

But instead of her emitting the high piercing shrill call that most did at such times, she sighed and withered, like a fresh rose blossom drying beneath a harsh desert sun.

He pulled away, not bothering to drain her fully. He pulled his pants up and drew his tunic over his handsome young chest.

He turned to the mirror before him, admiring himself.

"I will always remember you, my love," he mimicked her dying words to him, she not realizing they were to be her last as she succumbed to his vampiric embrace.

Though no vampire, the results were as dramatic, if differing in the outcome of the body. While his victims slowly lost their youth and vitality, his aging process reversed and he grew more vibrant, youthful, happy, and deliriously happy to be alive.

They, however, not until the last moments, ever realized that their climax of joy was also their nadir of life.

"I am so roguishly handsome, old chap, are I not?" He told his mirror image.

"Not even close," the image replied.

He gave it a shocked look.

A hand reached out and grabbed him by the throat. "Blaggart, how dare you waste our precious time here, when we much to do yet?"

Then he was drawn through the mirror in an explosion of light and energy.

Gargoyle

From a distance, she appeared to be just another gargoyle overlooking the park. She was close to one that was of a close height. It allowed her to continue hiding her acts of hunger from the ever-wary constables that roamed this part of London.

She smiled to herself. Fools! The living dead were ageless. They didn't stop learning the tricks of man. This is precisely why she kept evading them. They were wary, but she was clever. And clever wins every time!

She glanced at the shriveled mother lying at her feet and smirked. Nothing!

The baby made a cooing sound and reached for her face. "Not yet, sweetie. Mommy. Your new Mommy needs to eat first. I'm saving you for a snack."

The baby laughed happily and kicked.

"Oh," she laughed. "You are cute, aren't you?"

The baby proved it by laughing even more loudly and reaching for her nose again.

She nuzzled the hand with her nose, allowing it to play with it a moment, then wrapped the baby more to keep it safe and warm.

She laughed at the delicious humor of it. But she was serious only to a certain extent. She didn't intend to kill the baby.

She was fond of it because she had such gentle, green eyes. Like hers had been once...before Dracula had turned her in the early days before he changed.

She scowled at the memory.

"You ruined me!" She declared to his memory. But the anger flew away when the baby kicked for attention again, making more happy sounds.

She began to experience pain in her heart. How could that be? She had no heart to speak of. It had been drained dry by that evil Count. Not the live one now, but what had been an evil man. How could he just turn like that on his fellow beings?

The baby made sweet sounds, its eyes going droopy.

She felt the pain again. Then she felt something else new. Worry. She'd never worried about anyone else but herself, not even before the Count. But tonight, something had changed.

She looked into the baby's drooping eyes.

Yes. Yes. She was to blame.

So cute. So very, very cute.

Then something else new arose. Regret. How could she turn this small creature? So full of love. So sweet?

"Curse you Count!" She cried out beneath her breath.

The baby girl nuzzled against her breast, making little sucking sounds as if eating.

Her heart ached again.

"I must feed her!"

She kissed her forehead and laid the baby down against the gargoyle's feet, covering its face so the night breeze wouldn't bring a chill to its young body.

No, she wouldn't turn it.

She would keep it.

Raise it like her child.

Then she would need a name for it.

She smiled.

It would be safe to leave it now. It wasn't too cold. When she returned after her meal, she would return to the church basement where her bed of dirt was. In the night again, she would seek a nice flat for her and the child.

Yes.

That's what she would do.

Then her mind returned to the Count and his

arrogance again.

The old fool and his stupid contract with the Queen and her government. Didn't he know that vampires couldn't survive without human blood?

His nonsense about using animals for blood was revolting and sickening to her sense of values.

She and others like her were forming an underground resistance to his machinations. Soon, soon now. They would be ready to rise and overthrow him.

She laughed.

Her attention flew below to the park again. From here, where she stood, she could shop for new blood, which on the ironic side of things made the name Market Park...well, ironic, as it was her marketplace for restoring her strength and beauty.

And hopefully, the victim would have some money she could use to better her life now that would be shared with...Baby! *A perfect name*, she thought.

She poised as if before a mirror, seeing her human form. The one that the mortals would see tomorrow.

Her long red tresses fell halfway to her knees, overlaying her shoulders like a crimson cloak, hiding the pale skin that peeked out. Her lips were blood red, which suited how mortals perceived her. She enhanced them with cosmetics from the theater and underlined her eyes with thick black rouge.

Not for beauty in that case, but to give herself more of a shock value. Didn't want her to go screaming and running off. Then she'd have to chase after them which could turn nasty if a constable happened to be around.

She glanced at her left shoulder. It still had a silver burn there from a smart constable who added silver to the tip of his nightstick. If not for that, the young redheaded man would have been her snack that night. But now as she perused the park for late nighters, she saw something odd happening below.

"Ahhh!" She sighed with pleasure. "Dinner is arriving!"

Market Park Portal

"I find this version of London to be quite…quaint," Professor Moriarty commented as he and Dorian Gray stepped forth through a glowing portal situated between towering maple, oak, and walnut trees.

Traffic was light because of the hour, so the new Tesla vehicles and the noisier steam-driven ones with their huge propellers droning steadily, puffs of steam emitting behind the vehicles, was getting less. So even from Haightbeery Street Park and Market Grove Lane, which enclosed the park on both sides where they emerged, were pretty much hidden from their eyes, and the eyes of other humans from them.

No one noticed.

They wouldn't.

It was late.

Sleep was the route most were taking.

Though a twenty-four-hour city; still the majority worked the daylight hours, making their emergence less spectacular because none would see it.

They hoped.

But someone had.

She swooped down, fangs extended, eyes bloodlust red, clawed fingers outreached.

"Boring!" Professor Moriarty sighed and stabbed her with the tip of his cane, which was silver, through her heart.

She burst into flames.

"No!" She cried out. "My baby! Have mercy!"

Moriarty shrugged. "What is this world coming to when vampires have babies?"

She twisted the tip, so it pierced her heart.

She shrieked one last time, eyes flying towards that distant gargoyle where a small baby girl would never know a mother's warm embrace again.

And this moment she had another awakening. She had grown her heart back only to have it snuffed.

With that realization, Moriarty pulled his cane from her body and stepped back to watch as smoke erupted from her skin and then flames.

She smoldered several long moments and then collapsed into a poof of dry dust filtering to the ground.

"What a waste."

"Dear Dorian, would you have her spoil your lovely throat?"

"Of course not, but I would have loved to have done hers."

"Throat?"

"What else would I be talking about?"

Dorian kicked at the vampire's ashes and then sighed. He glanced at the trees about them and sniffed the air. "I had thought to have a snack once we came through the portal."

"Not all good wishes are fulfilled, old chap," Moriarty replied.

"Sadly."

"I'm quite certain that most of the good London citizens are more interested in their evening meal than in popping around a large park filled with shedding trees as fall butchers the green ones and splays them with golds, oranges, and red leaves."

"That's quite poetic!"

"I was an English professor at one time."

"What happened?"

"I lost interest."

"Sad. You might have become a great poet one day."

"Perhaps, but I could almost like this place."

Dorian primped his hair. "Almost?"

"I would like it more if it had a proper name," Professor Moriarty stated. "I find its name to be much too long."

"Oh?"

"Yes. Something simple like Park. Or Trees would suffice."

"But how would anyone tell one park from another if they were all named like that?"

"Who said all? Merely this one. Others could be Leaves or Trunk."

Dorian gave the man a blank look.

"Joking, old chap. Even I have a sense of humor."

"Hardly."

"Well, this evening I do."

"If you say so."

The Professor preened his hair a moment, what little there was of it. He had lost most of it in a fire that his mortal enemy, Sherlock Holmes, had caused him to fall into.

He licked his right forefinger to wet the lock of hair he liked to have hanging between his eyebrows. It hid the scar made there by that man he hated very, very much.

Holmes seemed to be the death of him in all worlds. Except for this one. And the last. This one would be different.

He smiled. He had learned from the debacle that some of his doubles had made here an earlier time, using his name's sake James Moriarty as a human sacrifice. They should have known better. The only one who can kill him is Holmes. And soon, he would continue the long... well, not really, it just seemed that way...long tradition of murdering every Sherlock Holmes that ever existed.

But before that, he intended to destroy every possible ally he might find in this world. And that would be not just interesting, but fun and...pleasurable.

His lean, wiry body twisted about easily in his dark suit, tie, and starched white shirt. He clutched an ornate cane with a goblin head for a handle and arcane symbols streaking its circumference to its gleaming silver tip.

He eyed the tip and reached down to clean it fastidiously with his jacket handkerchief. "Can't have the Count's blood on it. Might alert someone and cause trouble. I hear the Count here has many followers and as you know, dear Dorian, they have quite a sensitive sense of smell."

"Aren't you forgetting you've just slain a vampire?"

"Not at all. They leave no trace when they're shifted."

"But she was not shifted."

"True. But she was not a full vampire. Did you not her cry about the baby?"

"I did."

"That makes her mortal…even if a bit fanged."

"I see; that's why you're not worried about the smell exuding from the tip now."

"Not at all. Now the tip shall be both clean and smelling clean as well. Using a bit of dry vampire is the best way to cleanse blood odor too."

"Otherwise, they smell like death warmed over. Anything else must smell like roses to them," Dorian added with a slight twist of humor on his lips.

"I would laugh at the sheer nonsense of that, but I find it somehow quaint and true. Though the last Dracula wasn't too happy about the appellation, I'm sure the one here might find it simply appalling"

"Vampires deserve to die."

"They're already dead."

“Not the ones on this world.”

“Must you be so picky? We’ve managed so far to put an end to them on the other worlds.”

“Yes, we have, haven’t we? Quite a bit of fun that was.”

“Always. And surprisingly, it’s amazing how much younger I get when I absorb their life force.”

“Ironic though.”

“Why do you say that?”

“Well, since they live on the life force of others...”

“Well then, let’s see if we can’t help them undo that little error here as well, shall we?”

“I concur.”

“Kill them all are the right words, are they not dear Professor?”

“Why Dorian, one would think you like the infernal creatures by the way you remark upon them.”

“Then they would be using drugs or deluding themselves, as I hate them all!”

Professor Moriarty turned attention to the glowing portal behind them. “Shut!”

The portal closed with a pop.

“Why does it obey you like that?”

Professor Moriarty smiled condescendingly. "Should I tell you that, I would have to kill you, my dear and convenient partner."

Dorian growled. "I am a partner as long as we stay on task. You start seeking petty revenge as you did on the last parallel world, and I swear our convenient partnership will become quite ugly indeed and I will leave the way we came."

A long pause of tense silence.

"Without you."

"Really! And how shall you do that since I am the only one here with the touch of magic to open the portal?"

Dorian bit his tongue and looked away. Truth had a sharper bite than the look of old wrinkles returning on his Apollonic face. Wrinkles marred his classical good looks and he hated that more than death. He would rather die than look old and lose his good looks. Some called him a narcissist, but he saw that word as a means for those of marred appearance to try and hurt him. He ignored such nonsense.

Now he was aligned with a boorish man, who had no classically good looks. He looked more like a dried prune and his eyes would scare ten years off the life of a child were they to get up close. He hated the man. He was a low life he had to squander constant praise upon to gain a modicum of co-operation and respect. Simply disgusting was all he could think of the man. Was it not for the man's so-called touch of magic…?

His thoughts were shattered by a shout, thus saving him the necessity of prostrating his pride before the Professor.

"You there!"

He snapped to attention, turning in the direction of the hail.

A constable was heading for them, nightstick out. "What are you two blokes doing here at MidBells? Park is closed. No one allowed. Let me see your fire permit?"

"Fire permit?"

"Yes, I saw the fire you started."

"We started no fire."

The constable eyed them both, then the dust at their feet. He kicked it and the ashes rose in a twirl about their legs.

"Oh, that."

"Yes, that!"

"Some woman was making a fire to warm her baby."

"Where's the baby?"

Moriarty smiled. "She didn't say, and we didn't ask."

"And where's the mother?"

Dorian eyed the dust with humor. "One might say she dusted herself away, pardon the pun."

"Think you're funny, you two. Show me the permit or straight to the Yard with the lot of you."

Dorian grinned at Moriarty. "Please, do let me show mine first, Professor."

"Why certainly, my friend."

This, at least, was one thing they could agree in common upon. Being obedient to the law.

Dorian seized the constable's stick and hand so fast he didn't have a chance to back away.

"Let go or I'll have you in a cell for the rest of your miserable life!"

"Of which I shall have many more years, while you, constable. Your minutes are numbered."

"What rubbish!"

Then the constable looked at his hand.

Even as he watched it began to pop with blue blood vessels, brown age spots, then wrinkles that traced black and brown paths from his wrist, threading their way about his arm and then in a few moments, bursting like rotting flowers along his neck and into his face.

He began to lose height and bend over like an ancient man of many, many years, his hair retreating from his forehead, graying, and then falling away to reveal pure white hair that fell across his shoulders and then spilled like a swarm of desiccated snakes upon his shoulders and arms.

"What have you done?" The constable cried out in alarm, not comprehending what was happening, but feeling his life force being sucked away...faster and faster, while the man opposite him appeared to be standing taller, his eyes sparkling bright and clear, skin pinking with a vibrant new life. Hair growing thicker over his forehead, frown lines vanishing, cheeks growing vibrant with life.

"Merely removed an inconvenience," Dorian replied, not letting go.

"No!"

"Yes," Dorian replied nicely. "And yes indeed."

Dorian's face and hands continued to lose their age lines and wrinkles. As the constable aged towards death, Dorian aged towards his glorious youth.

Finally, he let go of the constable.

There was nothing more to take from the luckless man. "Thank you for your kind donation," Dorian stated with a sad kind of amusement.

The man collapsed in a heap of clothing and bone dust, as well as shriveled skin.

Dorian turned to Moriarty. He wiped a handkerchief delicately across his lips as if brushing off the crumbs of something he had just eaten. "That was tasty."

"Disgusting you mean. But efficient."

Moriarty raised an eyebrow. "Now that you've had your small revolting meal, shall we leave to perform more important matters?"

"After you…my convenient partner."

"What of the other?"

"We will deal with them when it is time."

They broke into laughter, strode from the park onto the sidewalk, leaving behind them the remains of the dead constable.

A strong, gusting wind blew in from the Thames and the dust-like remains of the constable fled into the air, joining in a sad dance of swirling dust with that of the vampire woman, Mariette. Perhaps both were even traveling in a kind of way to another world where such darkness and evil did not exist.

But for the moment the constable was no more. And would be no more on this Earth. Nor the woman.

Gargoyle

"What's this?"

A chimney sweep peered around a tall chimney he had just climbed from, finished with cleaning it. His face and hands were dark with burnt charcoal. He leaned forward and pried at the bundle of cloth on the rooftop.

A tiny hand reached out and clasped his finger.

He let out a yelp.

The baby cried.

"On me mother's dying breath!" He exclaimed.

He lifted the bundle and pulled away the cloth hiding the baby's face.

It began to cry.

"Nar, nar, wee one, don't you cry now"

He began singing a light Irish lullaby and the baby's eyes began to droop.

It fell silent.

Harrigan O'Malley smiled. "Oh, is me wife gonna like this night, begorra."

He hugged the baby to him and made his way to the chimney again, picked up his scaling hooks, ropes knotted for him to grip and broom, then headed for the exit door in the middle of the roof.

The baby opened its eyes again as he reached for the door.

She looked at him and he looked at her.

The expression on both their faces was so wonderful that they both broke into laughter.

That night Harrigan found the treasure he and his wife had been seeking over the hard years. They hadn't enough to adopt, nor the status. But tonight. Tonight, was a miracle.

The baby girl reached for his nose, trying to tweak it.

He laughed.

She laughed.

He left the rooftop to begin a new journey in his life. Whoever had abandoned the baby surely wouldn't miss her. He and his wife...they on the other hand...would always miss her.

The baby laughed again as he began his descent from the rooftop.

Yes, tonight was truly blessed.

221B Baker Street

Holmes naps in his easy chair near the fire, a new book by Jules Verne and H.G. Wells open in his lap.

Watson gently removes it and places it on the sitting-room table, placing a sheet of parchment paper, a bit frayed at its ends with tea stains across its right side into the spot where Holmes had stopped reading.

He picks it up again and lays it once more on Holmes's lap, a gentle smile on his face. Let Holmes figure out how this happened, he thinks with amusement.

Ms. Hudson, seated at the table, gives him a waggle of her finger, a grin on her face. She knows how Watson is always trying to trick Holmes into admitting a mistake or making one. Not to be mean. But to challenge him.

Finished in his little trick, Watson sits down next to Ms. Hudson. "Tell no one!" He whispers with the hint of a smile on his lips and sparkling eyes.

She shakes her head. "You two!"

She raises, stretches, and then yawns. "I think I'll be heading for dreamland as well, dear Doctor."

Watson nodded. "I rather fancied this time we've had together; you know."

She smiled. "Maybe we'll have more." She yawned. Got up. "But another time."

"Another time," Watson declared, rising also. He walked her to the staircase and then watched her until she had entered her flat.

She shut the door.

He started to turn when it opened again, and she smiled at him. "Another time soon?"

He smiled and gave her a half-bow and a happy nod.

She giggled and shut the door again. Her laughter warmed his heart so much that he immediately began to hum a tune he had quite forgotten until that moment. Bach had written it for his lover in France. Something about Lilacs and Roses and love in the clover of heaven.

"No!"

Watson started, spun around, immediately lapsing into silence. "Holmes?"

He rushed back into the sitting room.

Holmes had leaped from his chair, seized a fire poker, and looked to be stabbing at something. The book that had been in his lap had fallen onto the floor.

"Holmes!"

Holmes stopped, shuddered, and then replaced the poker on its rack. He turned to Watson. "I fear it was just a bad dream."

"But…"

"A very real, bad dream."

"And?"

Holmes came forward, his eyes half-veiled. "One that could very well be coming true even as we speak."

"Prophecy?"

"I pray not, my friend, because if so, then we face dark times indeed. The darkest of many a year."

Watson frowned. "Well, as long as there are scones in that future, I shall manage somehow."

Holmes laughed.

He clapped a hand to Watson's shoulder. "God bless you, John. You always know the right thing to bring me back to my senses. Not that I've ever left them, of course."

"Of course," Watson replied with a smile.

Holmes picked up the fallen book. He nodded to Watson, who gave him an expectant look. "And thanks for saving my place. Not that I would forget it."

"Of course," Watson replied, a sheepish look on his face.

Holmes gave Watson a loving tap on his shoulder as he passed him for his bedroom. "One of these days you'll catch me, John. Don't ever give up. I rather enjoy these challenges you keep creating."

Watson didn't say a thing.

He hadn't realized his friend was onto him.

"But how…?"

Holmes looked back. "Your footsteps have a crinkling sound on the right, because your night slippers are worn on that edge, and you pressed a sheaf of paper there to block the hole."

"Yes, yes, true. But what about the time…"

"You put the salt into my tea?"

Watson gasped.

Holmes grinned. "Ah, dear Watson. My dearest friend Giles, a childhood companion, used that same trick when I was in boarding school. I've learned to detect its smell by now by the way it changes the fragrance of my tea or coffee."

Holmes turned around again. "It's not as if it didn't happen enough times."

"Good night, Holmes."

"And you, Watson."

Offended

"Harold!"

Silence.

"Harold, are you listening to me?"

Harold pulls the covers over his head.

Maybe she'll go away.

The covers rip away.

Maude stands over him, eyes fuming, face bloody red with anger. "You get your blinking ass outta bed and go knock on our neighbor's door. Now!"

He gave her a look of utter disbelief.

"Are you deaf?"

"No, but why would I do that? You know our neighbor always goes to bed when we're getting up and takes a bath then," he grumbles. "And you hate it when I'm nice to any woman besides yourself."

"I will be even less nice if you do not do as I say. Do you believe that?"

"I do. But why should I bother the pitiful thing? God knows she never bothers a soul."

"Are you truly that deaf and dumb?"

Then he hears it.

Water?

His eyes widen.

The sound of water.

Soft, but steady.

Inside their bedroom?

What!

He peers over the edge of his bed.

The floor is flooded.

"Blimey!" He swears.

He jumps out of bed, sticks his feet in wet, sloshy slippers, and then splashes for the front door, Maude wading through the water after him.

"I'm going to sue her for everything she has," he swears. "Ruining my good slippers like this, she has. Blimey. I can live with her late-night noises and antics. After all. Young people must have time to grow out of their youth, but wet slippers! That's going too far, mind you."

"Right you are, Harold. Now you go and give her a piece of your mind."

He suddenly stops. Turns around.

"What you are stopping for. Go on now. Go on!"

He frowns. "What if she gets mad?"

"What if I get mad?"

Harold deflates like a balloon. "Right now. Give her a piece of your mind."

"Yours."

"Right. Yours."

Maude scowls, ignores his confusion. "And make sure she cleans up this mess; I'm not going to," Maude declares triumphantly.

"I seriously doubt she's going to be mopping anything, my dear. If I were her, I would already have packed my bags and slipped out of town. The landlord is going to murder her, even if you don't."

"You mean you."

"No, I mean you!" He managed to blurt out.

Maude gave him a look of utter shock. Before she could recover and make his life even more miserable than it already was, he grabbed the front doorknob and flung the door open.

Bad idea!

A flood of water sloshed inside,

The entire hallway had at least a foot of water in it and was building steadily.

And no wonder since there was a door to the stairway down the water, shut tight as a gnat's bottom and with no exit beneath it.

"Blimey!" he cursed as he waded out, getting his ankles wet as he plodded for the neighbor's door. "I'm going to kill her."

He stomped through the water for her door, sending tiny wavelets back and forth and side to side of him. Some splashed into his face.

He scowled deeply, mumbling angrily beneath his breath, but fearing his wife more than the water, he carried on.

He knocked on her door.

"Marie, open up immediately!"

No reply.

"What the hell, Harold"

"Not my fault," he automatically replied.

Bullmond, his next-door neighbor from the opposite side of the hall stood butt naked in the hallway, his huge hairy chest fluffed up like a teddy bear that had been beaten to a pulp. His long white whiskers drooped limply to his chest. His eyes were bloodshot and bleary.

Hell had three names this morning. Maude, Marie and Bullmond.

"What"

He turned fully to Bullmond, his other next-door neighbor. A well-built man who managed the heavy iron at the Thames Water Works, dared a quick scowl, knowing the man could bend him like a pretzel if he wanted, even if twenty years Harold's senior.

He grabbed Marie's doorknob. It wouldn't budge. He frowned deeply, and then returned his gaze on Bullmond.

"Harold, do something!" Maude screamed down the hallway.

"Doing!" He shouted back.

"Let me!" Bullmond demanded, shoving Harold aside. He grabbed the doorknob. A breaking sound of metal on metal.

He smiled. "Now. Let's find the underlying cause of this, shall we?"

He pushed on the door to open it.

Nothing.

Harold broke into a grin and immediately hid it when Bullmond scowled at him. "Bloody hell, she's barricaded the door!"

Hank, another neighbor peeked out from his room, water flooding inside as he did. "God's sake, what's going on here?"

Maude shouted. "The flood has begun."

Bullmond grunted. "Your wife's a bit off, Harold."

"Tell me something I don't know."

They both grinned at each other.

"Here, let's lean into the door together, Hank suggested.

They did.

The door opened slowly, and more water rushed out. The water stood almost to their chests as it rushed out in a tsunami flood.

"Mmm." Bullmond fingered his square, unshaven jaw, and eyed Harold. "I don't like this."

Harold tapped Hank's shoulder. "Hank, better get the constables up here quick."

"They'll need a boat," was the reply.

"You don't get down there right now, you'll need a coffin," Bullmond hollered.

Hank paled, nodded, and sloshed through the flood of waters to the door that opened downstairs. He leaned into it, and it opened, allowing a flood of water to follow him out and down as he descended the stairwell.

Then he noticed that the front entrance was flooded as well. The moment he dared to walk through water that was almost to his kneecaps, the landlord peered out from his doorway, almost swept off his feet by the tide of water he let in.

"It's flooded!"

That same moment the postal man chose to open the front door outwards to the flats.

Hank and Mister Dingles the landlord was swept out by the sudden rush of water, along with the postal worker.

They let out screams and cries as they were flung head over heels in a huge wash of water that drew them down the front steps and onto the sidewalk then the street, where a dog about to pee into the gutter, let out a yelp of terror and dashed for safety.

Once it had, it sat on its haunches, tongue lulling outside its mouth.

Hank sat up, saw the dog, and scowled at the dog. "The mutt's laughing at us!"

Mister Dingles sat up. "I suspect so."

Hank felt his head. He had banged it hard. "I need a doctor."

The sound of a constable's whistle.

Running feet.

They helped each other up.

Constable Reynolds reached them, eyed the pouring water.

"That bad, hey?"

Hank shook his head. "Worse. We can't get into a neighbor's flat. It's flooded."

"Why haven't you gone for a plumber?"

Bullmond in a moment of utter lucidity replied from the entrance to the flat. "Why hasn't she?"

Constable Reynolds felt rebuked and was about to respond when he noticed something odd about the water now pouring down from above.

It had a dark tinge to it.

He dropped to a knee and caught some on the tip of his night stick and then eyed it.

"Blood!"

They all looked at each other and then up at the flat whose window overlooked the street. Marie's.

Constable Reynolds broke the sudden silence by blowing his whistle.

Hard!

Over, over, and over.

Marie's Flat

Constable Reynolds, Bullmond, and Hank put their backs to the door and pushed with all their might while Harold and Maude, holding hands, stood close together watching them.

"I'm scared, Harold."

Harold put an arm around her shoulders. "Don't be. I'm here."

She began to cry. She buried her head in his chest. "I'm so sorry I've been so mean to you."

Bullmond eyed them with a blank look. He had seen this sort of thing too many a time. *What a strange world* he thought.

"Okay, on three," Constable Reynolds said.

"One, two…"

"Three!" They pushed.

Nothing.

"It's the water pressure from inside," Bullmond remarked. "Too much water still filling the room. Probably a busted water pipe."

Maude looked up. "Poor girl can't be well with that much water."

"She'll be all right, dear. You just wait and see."

Maude sniffled and snuggled closer.

"Someone please turn off that bloody water!" Constable Reynolds ordered.

Mister Dingles, who had been standing at the stairwell door nodded and rushed downstairs for the basement door to do just that.

"Again!" Constable Reynolds ordered.

The three men pulled back and then slammed into the door.

It barely opened, but enough for them to force it further. As they did more water came flooding out.

The door slammed shut on them.

"Bloody hell!" Bullmond yelled.

"God, it must be four feet deep in there!" Hank gasped.

No comments.

"Get back!" Bullmond ordered.

He didn't wait for anyone to budge.

He kicked the door with all his strength.

The door made a huge crackling sound and began to form cracks up and down and at angles from where he had kicked it with his booted foot.

"Get away from the door!" Constable Reynolds ordered.

Everyone dodged to the sides just as the door made a huge cracking, snapping, popping sound, and pieces of it shot forward like bullets, embedding in the wall opposite the door.

"Blimey!" Harold cursed.

A flood of water poured out, washing about them, and streaming up and down the hallway, deepening the standing water there even further.

"It's a bloody pond in there!" Bullmond cursed when the water had slowed enough and peered inside.

He stepped inside, followed by everyone else.

Harold took Maude's hand. "Best you wait here, dear."

She patted his hand. "When this is over, let's talk."

He gave her a surprised look.

"About what?"

"Harold, come give us a hand!" Bullmond ordered from inside.

Harold joined the others inside as they waded through thigh-high water, past a floating sofa, a comfy chair on its side, a dining table upside down, cups and plates floating, and a single doll with a red button nose. It had a happy smile drawn on its bland face.

And it was Oriental in shape and form.

"Peculiar," Bullmond noted as the doll floated past.

"What isn't?" Hank pointed out.

"Ms. Waters!" Constable Reynolds announced. "We're coming into your bathroom. Don't be frightened, we just want to know if you're all right."

No reply.

"To it men," Constable Reynolds ordered.

They shouldered the bathroom door.

It whined and complained as the wood groaned against the hinges holding it in place and the lock on the inside strained to break free.

Snap.

The bathroom door broke off its hinges, and slammed outwards, sending Harold back into the pond behind him.

The same moment as it did a new flood of water came out and with it a head.

Detached.

Eyes staring off in horror into nowhere.

Then a hand.

An arm.

A leg.

And then Bullmond screamed like a little girl.

Bloody Gutter

Holmes and Watson made their way through a crowd of onlookers.

Holmes peered at the street gutter where standing water was. Tinged red.

"Watson."

"On it."

Watson dropped back to put a knee to the curb and open his black bag which was always in his right hand. He took out a glass vial, opened it, and filled it from the red-tinged gutter water, then capped it, stuffed it into his black bag, got up, and followed Holmes.

He noticed a pack of wild mutts slurping at the gutter water. It was tinged deep red, and he could swear he saw something resembling an ear floating in it. But then a mutt snatched it up, and ran off, chewing on what it had found to keep the other dogs from having it.

But more peculiar was the odd doll that had been bobbing up and down next to the ear.

The mutts left behind scattered when Watson approached to pick up the doll.

He held it up to examine it closely.

"Chinese?"

He examined it further, turning it about slowly, and then sniffed it. "Interesting."

He shoved it into the black medical bag he always kept in his right hand.

Holmes held his silence. But Watson could tell something was bothering him.

"Holmes?"

"Nothing, Watson."

"I know better."

Holmes sighed.

"When I traveled to China…"

"What! Did you travel to China? When?"

Holmes's face turned unreadable once more. "Another time, Watson."

Watson grumbled. "Always another time."

Holmes smiled. Now was not the best time for that story.

Perhaps later.

His mind drew back to that journey and just as quickly retreated.

Another time as he had told Watson.

When they were both ready.

Bloody Bath

"Bloody nasty!" Inspector Bloodstone proclaimed as his men carried out the trunk and chest of a woman.

He had his men gather all the grisly body parts and reassemble them so that the now quite thoroughly dead Marie could have some resemblance of peace in death, if not life.

"Who would do something like this?" He asked himself, shaking his head in dismay and sadness. He had seen many an atrocity in his time, including that of Jack the Mad Ripper, but this...this...

He caught a movement near his right and turned. He nodded to the man waiting silently for his attention.

"Holmes."

"Inspector."

Holmes eyed the water destruction in the sitting room. "Death by drowning on the books?"

"For now. Don't want to alarm the public over what might be a one-time thing, do we?"

"Dismemberment. Perhaps a death sentence from some obscure cult?"

"Holmes, you're the detective on this case. You tell me."

"I will do some research once Watson has had a chance to thoroughly examine the remains. That should give us a clearer picture of what happened."

"I'll leave this to you and the doctor then."

"We'll get to the bottom of this."

"Sincerely doubt that, but you and the Doctor need to make certain of all the facts you can gather on the crime scene before me boys come to clean up the place."

"Agreed."

"How long?"

"Give us three hours."

"That much?"

Holmes looked the Inspector in the eyes. "I suggest you use that time to determine what story you are going to release to the press."

"What press?"

The sound of hollering came from outside.

The Inspector went outside and glanced out a window of the hallway.

Dozens of reporters stood below looking up as he looked down. They took pictures and held up notepads, shouting questions.

He hurriedly withdrew his head.

He turned about and almost knocked into Holmes.

"Convinced?"

Inspector Bloodstone gave him a sharp look. "How do you manage that? Creeping up on someone so quietly like that?"

"China."

"China?"

"You've been to China?"

"Some time back."

"Why?"

"As I said to Watson earlier, a story for another time."

"Watson doesn't know?"

"A story for another time," Holmes insisted, looking away, which annoyed the Inspector even more.

He frowned, but he also knew that once Holmes set his mind, he was like a rock. Immovable.

The Inspector frowned deeply a moment, bordering an explosion of anger, which he was prone to when stressed, then sighed in surrender. "Very well. I'll keep the horde entertained while you and the good doctor do your work."

Holmes nodded. He eyed the stretcher with the piecemeal Marie on it. "Watson is not going to like this one bit."

"And I do?"

"Point taken. But still, we need to know the original cause of death. I am not sure that clues we're going to find now will define the perpetrator. "

"But they might?"

"Might is a big word in this case."

"What do you mean?"

"I'd rather not say just yet."

"Why would someone drown a woman and then carve her up like a Christmas turkey? If not a cult, then what?"

The Inspector waited. Hoping that Holmes would not intimate that some kind of monster was involved. He hated the darker side of London. The dark magic and evil that went on had been worse than ever. While this case hadn't the looks of magic; it had every appearance of being attached to some kind of evil event...or intent.

Holmes clenched his jaw in thought. He had some ideas, but none were worth voicing now, except the one...which he had hesitated to speak to Watson of and now, the Inspector.

Instead, he rubbed his jaw. The whiskers were light there. He didn't need to shave yet. At his age, most men had a thick shadow beard and mustache. He had none nor ever would. The color of his hair diminished that possibility. And quite frankly, he didn't like the idea of shaving anyway, though he did somewhat to keep his facial hairs in check.

"I imagine this case will be a bit of a test for you, lad."

Holmes eyed the Inspector thoughtfully. "Perhaps. Perhaps not."

"The bathroom please," Holmes requested.

Constable Reynolds came forward at a nod from the Inspector "To the right and down three doors, Holmes," Constable Reynolds directed. "Follow me."

Holmes followed him to the open bathroom. He noted the splintered door frame.

"It took three of you to open the door?"

"How can you tell that?"

"There are impressions in the doorframe at three different points. A bit of cloth."

He plucked out a dark piece and held it up. "Yours I believe."

He then pulled two other pieces away, each a different kind of fabric and color. "The others?"

"Remarkable," Constant Reynolds gasped in wonder.

"Forensics science is much more precise than in its beginnings, Constable Reynolds. I'm quite sure one day that all I do, you shall also be doing."

He eyed the broken and dented portions of the door frame a moment in silence, eyes sweeping its edges for clues, then paused.

He dropped to the floor on his right knee and pried at something caught in the wall paneling there. He pried it loose with the help of his forefinger, and then lifted it towards his eyes to examine more closely.

"Mmmm."

"Mmmmm?"

Holmes stood. "I've seen this material before."

"Where?"

"China."

"You broke the door down because the water pressure on the other side was insurmountable. The only way to get in would be to break the door off its hinges, I presume."

"That's correct, but how can you tell that?"

Holmes chuckled. "Constable, it's not such a shocking surprise. The door frame broke where the hinges connect to the door. You would not have had to do that, were the door just locked."

"Oh."

"And the broken pieces do not go inwards as they should, if you broke the door in that direction, which you did. But the water pressure resisting your efforts caused the wood to shatter, thus making it appear to break from both directions.

"True. We did have to break it down from this side."

"Water pressure of course."

"Absolutely, but you already knew that."

"I did."

"But I have a rather odd question for you, Constable Reynolds."

"Yes?"

"If it was water pressure shutting the door, how is it possible for that much water to have built up from a simple bath?"

"I imagine…"

"And flood the flat."

"Well…"

"And the hallway to the stairs and below?"

"Water is like magic sometimes, the way it acts, I bloody well think."

"How likely is it that water would do this, Constable Reynolds?"

"Not bloody likely. But then the idea of a man or woman who sucks blood to stay alive is also bloody unlikely as well, is it not?"

"Point taken."

Holmes entered and saw a large oval-shaped tub with ornate dragons surrounding its edges and crawling along its legs.

"The woman was not oriental"

"No, she was not."

"I see."

The tub was anchored beneath the window of the bathroom. Still filled with water. The water was clear.

Holmes felt the water a moment, frowned, and then noted the bloody handprints on the wall, the windowsill, and the bathtub hot and cold-water knobs.

"Well then, it seems an easy enough job for the mastermind, does it not, Holmes?"

Holmes gave Constable Reynolds a light smile. "Perhaps. Perhaps not."

Watson burst inside. "What a mess! You should have seen the poor lass; her body was like a bloody puzzle made of flesh."

He froze at the sight of the blood and prints.

Holmes nodded. "What is obvious, dear Watson is that nothing is obvious."

Holmes held out a hand.

Watson pulled out a notepad and charcoal pencil. Holmes began sketching the bathroom.

Watson waited patiently, making notes for himself what Holmes was concentrating on, hurriedly writing them down on another pad of paper.

Something about the bloody fingerprints that didn't make sense.

To either of them, from what he could gather, Holmes's thought.

His eyebrows suddenly arched as Holmes turned about. He smiled. Noted the underscored words on Watson's notepad.

"Excellent."

"Through?"

"For the moment I am, but..." he gestured to Watson's notes. "I see you have come to the same conclusion, Watson. He put his sketch into Watson's bag. "We shall take a detour on the way home to the Museum."

With those words, he exited quickly.

Constable Reynolds turned to Watson with a question on his lips.

Watson shook his head. "Don't ask me. His mind is already into tomorrow. Enough for me to try and keep up with his today."

Watson hurried after Holmes, leaving a baffled Constable Reynolds.

Rooftop

Constable Reynolds stood alongside the Inspector as Holmes peered over the roof edge. A brick wall edged the top, allowing for a man to grip it and lower himself down the front face of the building. Falling from a series of slots in the roof edge were regular water funnels to catch rainfall and runoff to the street below.

These were slots in the wall for the deluge of water from the regular London swells that surged from broken cloud banks over London during stronger winter storms. They allowed orderly streaming of the overflow across the rooftop to pour to the sidewalk below and there to the gutter and the London sewers.

Otherwise, the standing water, which would sometimes rise as high as four feet if the rooftops allowed, would stand there, find every nook and cranny, and flood the interior of the building at the worst or the best inside the walls, causing mold.

"A man could scale these."

Holmes nodded. "A strong man could as there are no other points to grip and allow the climb."

"True."

"Odd thing though, Constable."

"Yes?"

"Seems to be scratch marks in the slots."

"Scratches?"

"Yes, very faint, but there, nonetheless."

Holmes examined opening after opening, then stopped. He took out his magnifying glass and leaned closer, then eyed what he had perceived as a possible clue.

"What is it, Holmes?"

"I'm not sure."

He put on his surgical gloves to protect the clues and gently probed at a slot made in the opening. He saw something interesting clinging to the slot.

"I need Watson."

"Right," Constable Reynolds said and dashed for the stairs to the flat below where Watson was working.

"What is it?"

Holmes turned a solemn face on the Inspector. "Unless I'm mistaken, it's guano."

"Guano? As in bat..."

"Exactly."

"Why would a bat leave it in that particular spot?" Bats prefer dark, shadowy spots. That slot would provide none of that."

"That remains to be seen. But there is more."

"Yes?"

"I believe someone may have scaled the building using the rain slots."

"A rather tiresome task."

"Yes, but it also coincides with the guano."

"Lot of bats."

"Or one bat leaving a path."

"Why?"

The Inspector raised an eyebrow in question, but Holmes was already making his way further along top of the building's roof.

Watson came running across the rooftop to join them. Huffing and puffing he waved a hand at Holmes. "I found something."

"As have I. You first Watson."

"Guano."

"And did you also find scratch marks at the windowsill of the bathroom?"

"How did you know that, Holmes?"

Holmes stood up and turned to look Watson fully in the face. He didn't say a word.

"And..." Watson was hesitant.

"And what? Out with it, Watson."

Watson swallowed hard. He gave the Inspector a long look, almost pleading. "I thought the vampire race was behaving themselves."

"They are."

Watson shook his head. "The young lady in the bathtub would seem to disagree. Sadly. Her throat...what we could find of it... has two puncture marks."

Holmes's eyes narrowed.

"You're sure, Watson?"

"Why would I make such a thing up?"

Holmes turned to the Inspector, who looked baffled. "Any other incidents of vampire attacks?"

"Not a one. Not since the Count moved into the city and made it illegal for the vampire race to intermingle and feed off humans."

"Indeed," Holmes said.

"Yes. And he has guaranteed it will never happen again. On his honor. And thus far..." He looked uncertainly at the roof top and what had been revealed about it. He looked up. "…I don't know what word to put to this. Quite puzzling."

"Why?"

"Why would such an honorable man…er, vampire…break his own rules?"

"We don't know that for certain yet."

"True, but the clues you've been revealing…"

"Again, are not conclusive."

"Still…"

Holmes nodded. Considered very carefully his next words. "Still, there is the possibility that our dear Count just might have had a change of heart, might he not? Or at the very least, one of his tribes."

"They are not called a tribe, Holmes."

"Swarm?"

Inspector Bloodstone shrugged. "Close enough."

Holmes paused and then turned to Watson. "Did you get samples of the guano?"

"I did."

Holmes indicated the one in the wall slot. "There as well, please."

As Watson stooped to retrieve the sample, Holmes looked at other rooftops about them, measuring the distance from one to the next.

"I shall need a team."

"At once. For what?" The Inspector asked.

"To examine the neighboring rooftops."

The Inspector turned to look. There were hundreds of rooftops in view. "All of them?"

"Indeed."

"What will my team be looking for?"

"Guano."

"Bat sheet?"

"And scratch marks nearby."

Inspector Bloodstone sighed and then nodded to Constable Reynolds. "Within the hour."

"Yes, Inspector. Bath crap and scratches."

Constable Reynolds rushed off at the Inspector's nod to gather his team.

Watson finished capturing the sample, placed it into his doctor's black bag and rose to face them. "What now, Holmes?"

"The Museum before it closes."

"It is often said that to judge a book by its cover is to miss the essence of the story, but sometimes the story is no more than the fancy etchings of illusion that decorate the front of the book."

-- Sherlock Holmes

British Museum

"And you're sure these are samples of true vampire scratches, Director?"

The Museum Director, dressed like a dandy, with cotton swirls about his throat, trouser bottoms, and shirt sleeves, tugged on a tie that equaled the fancy of the swirls and turned red in the face. "I am not given to describing anything less than the obvious, Detective Holmes."

Holmes nodded.

He eyed the amber block with the embedded marks in it. "I wish to take this…"

"Impossible! Nothing leaves this museum without the signature of the Queen…"

Watson handed over a signature.

The Director blushed deeply. "However, I will be more than happy to give you all the help you require."

Holmes smiled. "I expect nothing less."

He handed the block to Watson, and then returned his gaze to the Museum Director. "I will try not to damage it much."

"Much!" The Director cried out in alarm.

"Come, Watson, we must hurry to examine this more properly."

"Thank you, Director. You will hear from us when we are through with the case."

"When's that?" The Director hollered after Holmes and Watson as they hurried off.

"When's that?" He repeated as the two men exited the room.

Holmes turned to Watson. "Please forgive me, Watson, for my slight lapse in courtesy, but that man is a fop and arrogant. He required an adjustment in his attitude."

"What if he checks with the Queen?"

Holmes smiled. "I have it on good authority that she will say nothing."

"How did you manage that with me by your side and not seeing any such thing?"

"Let's just say it has something to do with that China incident and a certain professor."

Count Dracula's Castle

The mansion looked cheerful enough. But it still had too many green things that appeared to have been ignored or abandoned. The front gate opening into the broader area fronting the mansion was ornate with gothic heads of various demons atop the spiked spokes of it.

Watson shivered violently for a moment.

"Watson?"

"Sorry, Holmes, but the idea of entering a vampire's castle...even if it is called a mere mansion...is not exactly my cup of tea."

"Nor mine. But I need the measure of this man. See no other way of doing so than this."

"Nevertheless." Watson opened his black bag to reveal a silver dagger.

"Pray we do not come to such a turn in our investigation, Watson."

"Why?"

"Vampires do not die just because you stab them."

"In the heart."

"John," Holmes turned to look at his friend. "It also requires holy water and the cutting off of their head."

Watson shut his bag. "Won't hurt to try."

Holmes clapped a hand to his friend's back. "As I said."

"Pray we don't come to that," Watson finished for him and chuckled.

Holmes's right eyebrow arched in thought as he entered.

Then he stepped back.

The furthest spike of the gate had a blemish on it.

Watson saw his look. He nodded.

"You're quiet, Inspector."

"I don't know how to take half of the information that passes through your lips."

"Believe nothing you hear, and nothing you see and use your logic, and you should be fine, Inspector."

Watson laughed.

The Inspector scowled at him.

"Don't you have work to do," the Inspector scolded him.

Watson attended to his task of taking a sample again, but the smile remained on his face.

Holmes and the Inspector marched along the curving path from the front gate to the mansion's entrance.

Inspector Bloodstone nodded to Constable Reynolds, who had arrived ahead of them to scout the area. His men were waiting for his nod at the street, keeping behind cars and out of sight of the windows of Dracula's home.

Constable Reynolds jerked a hand down hard to signal his men. They scattered, a half dozen heading for the side of the house on one side and another half dozen to the other side of the house.

The remaining five followed Constable Reynolds behind Holmes and the Inspector. Holmes turned to both men and gave them silent instructions, which they nodded to him in return. This was carefully choreographed.

They stepped onto the porch and Holmes raised a hand to knock on the door. One would never know what he was thinking after the silent instructions he had given by the look on his face, but his eyes had hardened.

Something was wrong. He sensed it before he stepped onto the porch. He just didn't know what yet.

It opened before his knuckles could strike. A tall man, with clean-cut features, piercing brown eyes, stark black hair, and a long chin that seemed to come to a point, eyed him from inside the now open door.

"I've been expecting you."

"I see," Holmes replied. "And who exactly are you?"

Holmes felt the air about him become electric. He knew exactly who the man was. His aura was so intense that most men would fall prey to it immediately. This was no surprise to Holmes, considering the powers that Vampires had over most mortal men.

But he was not most mortal men.

His training in India and China had removed that part of him…forever.

The tall man eyed the Inspector next. Holmes felt as if an invisible hand was removed from about his throat. "Inspector."

The Inspector froze.

His feelings about the encounter were no less intimidating to him than it had been to Watson just at seeing the home.

The Tall Man, seeing he would get no reply, turned back to Holmes, and gave him an elegant and smooth half bow.

"Please do enter my humble home."

He straightened. "You have my promise that no harm shall pass to you here."

Holmes gave the tall vampire a slight smile. "I would expect no less from such a distinguished man as you, Count Dracula."

"And I from you, Detective Holmes."

The electricity between the two men at that moment was so intense that both Constable Reynolds and the Inspector backed up a bit, almost as if they expected lightning to strike.

Sitting Room

Watson elbowed past a servant who was as pale as a ghost with fangs hanging over his front lips. "I can see myself in, thank you."

He hurried past the foyer into a long hallway leading to the sitting room. As he did so, he passed silent vampire servant after another. Each looked straight ahead, but he could feel their eyes and stares upon his back as he passed.

He wished he didn't feel it, but he did. A kind of hunger followed their gaze.

He didn't give them the benefit of fear or shivers, which he surely felt to the tips of his toes at that moment. He held back the shiver of disgust he felt. Vampires were not his cup of tea. Polite or not.

As Watson passed along the main corridor to the sitting room, he noticed painting after painting, masterfully done that portrayed noble men and women. But the exception which drew another desire to shiver violently were the fangs that were painted in crimson that hung from their lips.

"Bloody vampires!" He muttered, hating having to be where he was; but not letting anything stop him from performing his duty and executing his friendship with his partner, Holmes.

Watson shuddered. Family portraits no doubt, but what a family! But part of him had to admit that the creatures had some sort of feelings, even if their…shall we say…appetites pursued a different course of satisfaction.

Vampire art was not his cup of tea either. And family portraits of vampires even less so yet. But he was not one to judge the habits or mannerisms of others, even those he despised unless he was forced to by their trespass upon his loved ones or fellow citizens.

He paused before entering the sitting room to glance at one more portrait. Obviously of the man who had let them in. It showed him holding a black bible of sorts over the heads of a crowd of vampires who had their heads bowed to him.

The meaning was obvious.

He was their master.

And they'd better obey or else!

The Sitting Room

Watson entered the sitting room, where another servant was pouring hot tea into cups for the seated men there.

Count Dracula nodded to Watson. "We were waiting for you, dear Doctor. I had an extra pot of tea warmed up just for you. I trust that will be to your satisfaction?"

"Dracula, I presume," Watson fired back, not happy with the look he was getting. He wanted to dislike the man but found it harder to than last exchange between them.

"Count to those who are not my friends."

"Count."

Dracula smirked at Watson. "So be it then. But I hope that in time we might engender a more, shall we say, a more enlightened attitude."

"Don't count on it."

A long pause.

"Count."

Dracula turned to look at Holmes, whose face remained poised in thought, which even the elder

Dracula could not read. He had to admit that Holmes was almost as fathomless to read as himself at this time.

He did the equivalent of a sigh and then nodded approvingly as Watson sat next to Holmes, who offered him a fresh cup of tea. They might not be friends…. yet…but neither were they enemies.

Watson peered into his teacup as if examining it for poisoned leaves, or jagged metal; something to kill him or at the least bleed him for a healthy meal for the blaggarts here, but he saw none of that. Instead, his nostrils flared with pleasure as they scented a fragrance he had not had the pleasure of experiencing for many years since…

"China?"

He looked up, giving the Count a surprised look.

"I had heard of your time there."

"You know a lot about the two of us."

"I make it a point to understand my…" He paused a long time, glancing from Holmes and then back to Watson. "…Friends and my…" He cocked an eyebrow at the Inspector. "Enemies?"

Watson got it.

The Inspector did not.

Holmes smiled. "A man after my own heart."

"I prefer blood to meat," Count Dracula joked.

The Inspector cringed. He was so creeped out that he could barely taste the tea he drank, even though it was excellent.

Watson took a tentative sip of his tea. His eyebrows rose. He eyed the Count. "Marmalade sugar?"

"Only the best for my guests," Dracula replied and seemed to be waiting for more by the hint of a knowing smile on his face.

"You're the first person to know my taste in sugars. Not even Holmes knows that. I acquired it in the China Wars."

"I know."

"But how could you...I've told no one of that time...not even my dear friend, Holmes."

The Count gave Watson an enigmatic smile. "Let's just say that I have friends in high...and low places and leave it at that."

Holmes took it all in, remaining quiet as the two discoursed.

"Interesting. You know my history?"

"I make it a point to know the histories of my friends...." Here his smile hardened a touch. "...And of my enemies...if you don't mind my repeating myself."

"I do not," Holmes replied with a dash of humor in his tone. "I would respect you much less were you to do anything less."

"Perhaps there is hope for our relationship, then, Detective Holmes?"

"I've seen stranger worlds than this."

"So, I've been led to understand. I would enjoy hearing of your other world."

Holmes took a sip of his tea and then nodded. "You play chess?"

"I have a modest ability I've honed over the centuries."

"Perhaps over chess some night."

"Holmes!" The Inspector interrupted, getting increasingly anxious as servants gathered at the several doors of the sitting room to watch silently, fangs hanging over their lips.

"Sorry, Inspector. But it's never good to insult a host over tea."

"I heartily agree," the Count concurred. "Speaking of which…" He turned to Watson. "I understand you have a sweet tooth for scones."

"How did you…never mind. Friends in places."

The Count smiled and nodded.

The Count smiled. "If you wish, I can have my servant bring you some blood scones."

Watson looked alarmed.

Holmes laughed.

"Watson, he's merely teasing you. Blood scones are a rare delicacy imported from Scotland. My father used to serve them for breakfast to my family."

"Oh!"

Dracula nodded with pleasure. "I am well acquainted with your perfect memory, but your family history remains quite lost to me."

"As it must."

Dracula nodded. "I understand. One never knows when information can be turned against oneself. And one's family are the most precious gifts that God can ever give us."

For a moment Count Dracula looked as if to cry, tears forming briefly in his eyes. He sniffed and wiped them away. "Please forgive me. I forgot to blink my eyes sometimes and they begin to water. God knows I try to remember but being a vampire, one tends to forget such mortal mannerisms."

"But of course, dear Count," Holmes replied.

Watson, sipping more tea, suddenly began choking on it.

Holmes patted him on the back.

"Watson, you alright?"

Watson wiped his mouth and face hurriedly. "Pardon me, Count, did you just say God?"

"Should I not have?"

"But twice...and..."

The Count smiled. "And I am still whole of the body and not turning into fire and smoke at the mention of the word"

"Vampires are supposed..."

"...To be afraid of God. Burn like a bush in flames by the merest mention of His name. I think not. That is just one more fairy tale with little truth in it, Doctor."

Watson set his cup down and rose.

He had a look on his face that Holmes recognized immediately and loved him even more for it.

"It would seem I am in debt for your obvious forgiveness of my former rude behavior."

He slowly reached his hand out." Please accept my most profound and utter apologies, Count Dracula. I mean it sincerely."

Dracula rose, gave a half bow, and then accepted Watson's hand, placing his other over theirs to clasp it more warmly. "And I accept your very generous and humble apology, dear Doctor. Perhaps that bit of a distance to our friendship has been diminished somewhat."

Watson grinned. "How many blood scones did you have in mind; I am a bit hungry?"

Holmes and Dracula broke into polite laughter at the twinkling in Watson's eyes and the utterly innocent and look of supplication on his face.

The Inspector tensed.

None of this was going the way he had expected it to. But he bit his tongue, biding his time. Holmes was never one to act in an orderly manner that was totally without surprise.

The Count clapped his hands and the servants all vanished.

The Inspector lost some of his tension, but Holmes noted that though they had vanished from the room, their shadows remained outside the entrances.

Unacceptable

"I apologize again for my rudeness. No crude vampire would ever serve a breather hot tea with Marmalade sugar and offer six sweet…uh…what did you name these?"

"Blood scones."

"Yes, dear Count. Exactly."

Watson glanced at the plate before him. Only one scone was left. It had a raspberry glazed exterior and a trail of fresh raspberry juice leaked from its sides making it sticky, but still warm, and all the tastier.

Watson glanced at Holmes who looked away with a smile as if saying "I won't tell!"

Watson scooped up the last scone to eat.

Count Dracula half bowed. "Well then, since we have come to an amiable portion of our meeting, is there more which we need to discuss?"

Holmes glanced at his partner, who was in heaven as he sucked the dribbling juices from the last scone before polishing it off with several huge bites.

Holmes stood up. "I'm afraid so, my dear Count."

"So soon then?" The Count asked in mock surprise.

“Watson?”

“I can’t be certain of course without a full analysis, but yes.”

Holmes turned to the Inspector. “It seems we have a solution to your question, Inspector.”

The Inspector, who has been watching everything from the entrance to the room, silently taking in the whole discussion and battle of the wits, stepped into the light of the huge fireplace, causing his already ruddy face to glow even redder, casting glittering highlights across his fierce red mop of hair.

Dracula acted as if everything were normal, but Holmes could tell the man’s brain was already divining everything that had happened inside and out into various patterns that would soon come together in a larger course of action to which he would not only be the witness but possibly the victim.

“What would that be?”

Holmes turned to eye the Count sternly.” The murder of a certain young lady named Marie.”

Dracula rose as if to think better.

Everyone in the room except for Watson stiffened, but Holmes relaxed when he noticed the Count winking at him.

"I don't recall the name."

"Perhaps you know someone who does?" Inspector Bloodstone asked in a stern voice.

"Perhaps. But not at this moment."

"That is too bad."

The Inspector glanced at Watson, then Holmes. "You know what I must do, of course."

They both nodded, though Watson looked away and gave the Count a look of utter sympathy.

Not lost on the Count, who remained gentlemanly and standing, hands clasped behind his back as if waiting for an event.

And it did not take long to manifest.

Constables flooded into the sitting room from three different directions, huge silver net clasped tightly between their hands.

"I assume this means you presume me to be involved in something...unseemly with this woman named Marie?"

Inspector Bloodstone scowled. "All evidence points to you, Count Dracula. We must place you in custody, willing or not, for the murder."

"And if I am innocent?"

He glanced at Holmes, who seemed a bit uncertain for a moment, but finally said, "I fear you have made a grave error, Mister Holmes."

"Perhaps. Perhaps not," Holmes replied, rising from his seat.

The constables remained surrounding the Count.

"Will you come of your own volition?" Inspector Bloodstone asked.

"I would never refuse a polite offer...of anything," the Count replied, the smirk lost for a time, resurfacing on his handsome face.

As he was led from the sitting room, he turned to Holmes. "I trust that one day I can earn your friendship as well, Detective Holmes."

"Perhaps. Perhaps not."

The Inspector scowled at him. "If you have another day left to do such!"

The Count nodded, a smile touching his lips. "Stranger things have occurred. Perhaps I shall find something that pleases your taste as well as I have our dear Doctor here."

Watson blushed.

The Inspector made choking sounds as if he had swallowed something the wrong way.

"I highly doubt it!" He snapped.

"Perhaps. Perhaps not," Count Dracula echoed Holmes. "May I walk out without the shameful disgrace and pain of silver chains?"

Holmes glanced at the Inspector, whose face was tight with anger and suspicion, but on Holmes's nod, he relented with a sigh. "Very well then, Constable Reynolds, we have his word. If he betrays it, you know what to do. If he tries anything, chain him!"

"We'll meet again, Holmes."

Holmes nodded to the Count. "Perhaps sooner than later."

The Count smiled and then joked, "Perhaps. Perhaps not!"

The Count was led out.

The Inspector turned to Constable Reynolds, "See to it that every inch of this house is scoured."

"What about the other...?"

He nodded to the vampire servants, who stood motionless near the giant fireplace that was now dark and cold.

"Have they made any effort to stop our men?"

"None, sir."

The Inspector turned to the servants. "As you know the Count has an agreement with the Good Queen Mary of Scots. Therefore, we shall leave you on your cognizance, but should any further deaths occur...of a blood nature...we shall return."

They just stared at him.

The Inspector exited.

A screaming came from outside the sitting room a few moments later.

A Human Error

Count Dracula screamed, howled, and clawed desperately at the silver chain net that was wrapped about his body now. His clothing was smoking, as if about to catch fire, his skin boiling like hot water, eyes bloodshot red and bulging out.

Claws extended from his fingertips and fangs out, gnashing at the silver and talons ripping at the silver, he struggled to break free. It took all twelve constables tugging in all directions to keep him contained.

Still. The more he struggled, the worse the burning became.

"Unchain that man!" Holmes commanded as he and Watson came into sight of the tortured Count.

The constables gave him a surprised look.

Holmes ignored them and grabbed the silver net covering the Count and tossed it to the ground.

He turned to the Inspector who came up with a surprised look on his face. "Who ordered this?"

"Not I! I was with Constable Reynolds, checking another room for evidence."

Holmes glanced at the constables. One looked away but finally cleared his throat when the Inspector fixed his attention on him as well. "My grandmother was struck down by a vampire. I..."

He looked down at his feet. "I shall resign in the morning, Inspector."

Count Dracula stepped towards the man. "I grieve for your loss, constable. I truly...do."

The constable looked up and then his eyes widened in surprise. Dracula had tears in his eyes.

"You're crying!" The constable said.

"You think because I am of the night that I am bereft of all humanity. I am not. I would feel no less if my mother were torn from my breast like that."

He reached out and touched the man on his shoulder and gripped it warmly. "Let me know where this happened, and I shall make sure the blaggart is caught and punished appropriately."

The constable broke free, but not with malice or anger. He turned away because he was crying. Touched by the sincerity of the Count, who truly meant every word, he said.

Not lost on Holmes or Watson as they took in the scene.

The Count turned to the Inspector. "Please, I beg you in the name of God and all that is holy, that you do not punish this man for the sins of my ancestors."

"We'll see," the Inspector replied, a stubborn streak rising at the idea of being told what to do by a...a vampire!

"Inspector, I wish to take back my earlier observation."

The Inspector and the Count both turned to look at him. Holmes's eyes were on the Count. "By all that is logical, this man should be guilty as charged. Watson never makes a mistake."

"True," Watson added.

"But this time he has."

"I say, Holmes, that's rather discouraging."

"Sorry, Watson. Sorry, Count. I had to know."

"Know what?" The Inspector demanded, getting more frustrated by the moment.

"Whether a vampire has a heart."

The constables about him broke into laughter.

Holmes eyed them. "How many of you would have forgiven the man who accused you of a murder you didn't commit?"

They stopped laughing.

Holmes turned to the Inspector. "I feel we are making a dreadful mistake by taking this one inch further."

"Holmes, I admire your tenacity to holding onto the truth," the Inspector replied, his mind made up. "But the law must be satisfied. You and Watson both said that the samples were those of the Count."

"Yes, but…"

"Therefore, the evidence is indisputable!"

Holmes stepped so very close to the Inspector that his men reached for their weapons.

"He offered no harm!"

"He's the killer…" Inspector Bloodstone blurted out thoughtlessly, but with force.

"Perhaps. Perhaps not!"

"But…"

"Inspector, I have offered my services to Scotland Yard repeatedly this last year in earnest, requesting nothing more than a fair wage in return. Many times, risking my life and that of my good friend, Watson."

"For which we thank you most sincerely."

"But…"

He stepped so close into the Inspector's face that the man blanched in fear. "If you ever, ever let one of your men mistreat the Count before this case is over with, I swear I will not only never work for you again, but I will go immediately to the Queen and demand you be removed from your office."

"But…"

"Am I clear?"

"But…"

"Are we or not…clear?"

The Inspector tossed his red mane of hair in frustration eyed Constable Reynolds who looked away. "Very well. You have my word."

Holmes smiled. "Like the good man I know you to be."

The Inspector sighed. Holmes kept him spinning like a top.

Holmes turned to the Count as he passed him with Watson.

"I will never forget this act of kindness, Holmes."

Holmes paused a moment to look at him, then said with a tone that brooked no misunderstanding. "Don't make me regret this!"

He and Watson stormed off,

"I fear you've made an enemy and a mistake, Holmes."

"Nonsense, Watson. The Inspector is within his rights to disagree with me, but not to be inhuman. Our ability to be humane is all that keeps us from falling across the line that separates light from the darkness."

"Don't you mean animal from human, Holmes?"

Holmes stopped. "Animals have no free will. Man does!"

They kept walking.

Holmes felt eyes upon him as he left. He smiled. The trouble with the law sometimes was that it became a law onto itself and exploited inhuman boundaries, instead of the more humane ones.

While he had no love for vampires, any more than Watson. He could perceive they also had souls and feelings. Yes, some had crossed the boundaries of healthy behavior. But not all. The Count had just once again shown that even among vampires, there was honor, courage, and kindness.

And most importantly...humility!

The Count would have much to think about as he waited for resolution of what he had been accused of.

Holmes didn't see the look on the Count's face. He didn't have to. He knew the man...for even a Vampire has a soul...was smiling.

He suspected that the Count was wondering how they might interact together in the future.

Whatever it might be, Holmes knew the outcome of it would be of benefit.

To both.

And unknown to the two of them at the time, a friendship was being born. But whether that would blossom eventually into a brotherhood of companionship between men and others that could never be broken that remained to be seen.

Ms. Hudson came into the sitting room with a large tray in her hands.

Watson jumped up immediately to give her a hand. "Here, let me help you with that."

"No need. I'm used to it."

Watson helped anyway. "No lady should be burdened by a man's unwillingness to lend a hand."

She looked away and he savored the clean lines of her gentle face, her well-coiffed hair, the starch of her blouse and skirt, the small lines of her ankles barely perceptible, hiding tiny feet he was certain were as beautiful as the rest of her.

She was a lovely woman in so many ways. Of body, spirit, and heart.

And in such moments, he felt his heart-stirring as it hadn't since…

He should never have traveled into that dark alley after so much light had shone upon his heart. At once he felt distraught as memories of his lost love strode forth boldly and plunged him into the depths of long despair that had not yet healed itself.

But even as he was attempting to shore up the defenses of his heart once more, he was not able to see that he had set himself upon a different course in his life. That it was branching off and that he had just struck a major point on his behalf with the young woman, their landlord, who was slowly warming to their friendship and returning a blossom of hope and love he had felt he might never find again.

Her eyes lit up a moment and her lips were caressed by a warm smile before she nodded to Holmes, who was watching with interest.

"Will there be anything else, Mister Holmes?"

"Not immediately. But I am expecting a visitor in about an hour. Will that be too late for you? If so, I can have Watson or I attend the door."

"None whatsoever. I usually spend an hour or so before retiring for the night."

"Oh?"

"Yes." She looked at Watson as she said it. "I love children. I knit clothing for my nieces and nephews."

"How sweet!" Watson declared and immediately blushed.

He hid his blush by immediately loading his dinner plate with small potatoes. "Really. I love knit garments.

They are so much warmer and comfy than a starched shirt or suit and tie."

"But you look so wonderful in your suit and tie, Doctor," Ms. Hudson blurted out so quickly and without thinking that she blushed with embarrassment. Now. She didn't mean it to come out that way.

Holmes smiled at the play between his friend and Ms. Hudson with a glow of warmth touching his heart. He liked them both.

Much.

Watson didn't notice. He was eyeing the scones she had included with the meal. He was about to plunge one into his mouth. "Ah, the aroma of this scone is delightful."

Ms. Hudson quickly replied. "I've got more downstairs."

Watson looked up. "Oh, I wouldn't want to deprive you."

"Not at all, Doctor."

And before Watson could see the new blush on her face, she fled downstairs.

"I rather fancy this woman, Holmes," Watson declared, totally unaware of the intensity of his statement and its intent.

"Indeed," Holmes replied, his hands steepled to his chin, eyes shut in thought. "I hadn't noticed."

Watson laughed. "You notice everything, Holmes."

Holmes smiled. "Perhaps."

"What's going on, Holmes. You've been quiet ever since we returned."

"The analysis came back, did it not?"

"You should know. You were first to the door to retrieve it."

"Indeed, I was, wasn't I?" Holmes asked in a distracted way.

He settled into a chair at the table and forked some vegetables onto his plate and began eating them. "Ms. Hudson makes divine boiled cucumbers and celery."

"Indeed, she does."

"And her tomato cheese omelets are superbly delicious."

Watson eyed Holmes suspiciously. "What are you up to, Holmes? You never discuss our cuisine."

Holmes dabbed a napkin to his lips and smiled. Then he rose and went to their coat rack, grabbed his hat and cloak.

"I think I shall take my evening walk."

"But you haven't had your meal yet."

"Please have Ms. Hudson keep them warm for me. I shouldn't be gone too long. Before our guest arrives, I suspect."

"Very well. Want me to come with you?"

Watson had a scone near his lips as he asked. Holmes smiled. "I think you are busy enough at the moment, thank you."

"Holmes!"

Holmes finished dressing in his cape, coat, and hat took an umbrella, and turned.

"The Count?" Watson asked, suspecting the reason of Holmes's sudden departure. "This is not over yet, Watson. Not by any definition."

With those parting words, Holmes sped from the room and hurried down the staircase and out the front door.

Watson immediately set his scone down and went to the window overlooking Baker Street.

"Did you two solve the poor girl's murder case?"

Watson turned to face Ms. Hudson. She had six more scones on a platter for him.

"I hope not!"

And with those final words, he allowed her to set the platter down before his plate, then gently caught her arm and pulled her to a chair next to him.

"If you don't mind, Ms. Hudson, I do so ever much love to hear about children."

Her eyes lit up.

"You do?"

"Indeed, I do! Perhaps you could enlighten me more about the garments you are making for them, who the children are, and what they mean to you?"

She smiled and without thinking took his hands in hers and excitedly began, "Well, for my first nephew…"

Cold Room

Doctor Jarvis came into the room alongside Inspector Bloodstone, who looked weak and weary but braved it anyway. A case is a case. You can't just walk away, not when another murder might be looming.

He and the Doctor immediately saw Holmes at one of the steel tables, mixing chemicals. He finished pouring a blend into a test tube and held it up for the two of them to see.

"Doctor, you found both guanos, even as Watson to be the same did you not?"

"I did."

"And did you take a new sample from the Count since his internment?"

"I have."

"May I have it please?"

Doctor Jarvis went to cold storage and extracted a sample held in a test tube. He shut the storage and returned to Holmes with it.

"Thank you, Doctor."

Holmes took the test tube and poured the same chemicals into the one in his hand. His eyes narrowed, brows furrowing in thought as he waited to see what reaction might occur.

The Inspector and Doctor both edged closer as the sample began to boil. As it did so, the color changed slightly from that of the other sample. Then it did an abrupt brightening.

Holmes immediately hurled the test tube towards the far wall, spinning about to take both men to the floor.

An explosion of fierce light and heat flared momentarily and then dissipated.

The three men slowly stood as ashes rained down on their shoulders.

"What in God's name was that about?" Doctor Jarvis asked, his face ashen white.

Inspector Bloodstone looked at Holmes. "I'm on it," he said and hurried out.

Holmes examined the far wall and the shattered shelving and storage units there.

"Only one thing could do this."

"What?"

Holmes turned to look the Doctor full in the face.

"I am not free to speculate just yet, but I will say that we should both pray it is not what I suspect it to be."

"Which is what?"

"The greatest danger to our freedom that humanity has ever faced."

"How do you know this?"

"Because the man claims to be the reincarnation of Genghis Khan and is the terror of China."

"Claptrap!"

Holmes looked away at the smoking wall.

"Perhaps. Perhaps not."

The Street outside Scotland Yard

A tall figure, face hidden by a silken hood, wearing a long silken gown with dragon symbols on it, watched as a second story of the building lit up brightly for a moment.

No one could see the expression on the figure's face. But if they could have, they would have seen a smile.

A triumphant one.

Get a Free Book from me.

Learn more about my Sherlock Holmes in the back of this book in the glossary. It will help you to understand the new world I have placed Sherlock Holmes within and those he deals with.

I describe most of my characters and the world the new Sherlock Holmes solves his cases.

Grab a free Sherlock Holmes book on me!

Request for Review

If you found some pleasure in reading my work, please take the time to leave a review for it. Authors can thrive or die for the lack of reviews.

Thanking you in advance for your kindness.

The Author

Author's Note

I've always had a great love for mystery and adventure. Starting with Agatha Christie's The Bat and ranging to Edgar Rice Burroughs Tarzan of the Apes and Jules Verne's Journey to the Center of the Earth.

It was only a short step between those three writers to run into Sir Arthur Conan Doyle and his wonderful Professor Challenger adventures.

I first read Sir Arthur Conan Doyle's wonderful spread of detective stories when I was still a child. I didn't own books, so I read them at the public library or my school library. There was no Internet of Things, no Internet at all at the time. I was very into books as a child, always a loner of sorts. Even though I loved people, I was somehow always more in love with books. Call me bookworm then. Now bookworm writer. Maybe.

I went through the entire adult library in my hometown as a child, reading everything from fiction to non-fiction, science fiction to fantasy, and classic literature to modern. It didn't matter. It was words on paper. I loved the smell of books. Still do, even though I cater to electronic books currently.

This is all a back-story of sorts to give you an idea of why my Sherlock Holmes while based somewhat on the canon of Doyle, is nevertheless much more than that. What would be the point of repeating what's already been done?

No, rather I saw this writing experience as an opportunity to allow my imagination to romp in his playground but take elements from other famous authors and stories I've loved over the years.

There are copyright issues when it comes to living authors, so even though I'd love to play in their yards too, that is forbidden territory. So, I have contented myself to take my love of classic literature...Doyle, Verne, Wells, Dumas, Shakespeare and pour them into a mutual melting pot. Kind of a United States of Literature, so to speak.

Whereas the Sherlock Holmes of Sir Arthur Conan Doyle functions out of London, England in the Victorian period; mine exists in a parallel world where all the authors who have ever lived and all their characters are alive at the same time.

Therefore, if you see me including Houdini and Sherlock together, Challenger and Conan Doyle, it makes more sense if they were alive in that world and not this one.

As a person with a strong scientific background...I wrote a treatise on reaching other dimensions (parallel worlds) as an 8th grader, which my Physics teacher was knocked out about...I believe quite strongly in an unlimited universe, where an infinite number of parallel ones/dimensions exist at the same time.

When I was in India, I found that some there adhere to the belief that everything that man can do or imagine exists in a vast cosmic tapestry so that we do not so much physically exist, as mentally/spiritually move through that infinite tapestry, each choice we make...right or wrong...creating a branching point that we must follow, even though there were already an infinite number of other ones. Remarkably close to the parallel world/alternate dimension approach that many scientists are now coming to accept as a reality.

When I was a kid, the scientists barely believed in 4 dimensions...length, breadth, height, and time. Now as an adult there is talk of at least 9 known dimensions.

But getting back to my stories, what makes them relevant and different is that I can populate them with any science, any character, any famous figure, writer, artist, or whatever and they all fit! They fit because I created them. For fun. For pleasure. To be able to play on a field of dreams with no end in sight.

So, as you read my stories, dear reader, keep in mind that the Tesla car in my story is not Elon Musk's electric car, but a vehicle invented by collaboration between Thomas Edison and Nicolas Tesla in my invented world. It runs not by electricity as we know it, but by different energy discovered by Tesla.

In my world, Sherlock Holmes is not the first one of the stories, but one of several. Watson, likewise. Just as Spock was duplicated in the Star Trek series of movies to continue their worthy stories, so have I decided to include devices that will stimulate our imagination, take us to places we could never have gone before, and allow me to interject from time to time some of the wonderful insights I have been honored to receive as a maturing adult. So, death exists in my creation, but it has many permutations and outcomes. All exciting and mysterious.

Following this is a description of major characters, as well as items used exclusively in my Baker Street adventures.

Glossary of the Baker Street Universe

A list of players, places, and things that take place in the Baker Street Universe created by this author as the playground for his fantasies...and hopefully your own as well.

Bollocks...A common word used by the British to indicate something was nonsense, trash. An expletive.

Blaggart...a disagreeable person.

Drat, dratted...A swear word like damn to indicate frustration.

Pahalgam...A region of India at the foot of the Himalayas, next to the River Ganges. Very small village.

Ragamuffins...Homeless children that help Holmes out and whom he supports to keep off the streets.

Tosh...Sheer nonsense and an unkind reference to the upper class at that time.

Tesla Car...The device was built by Ford in collaboration with Nicolas Tesla. Powered by a new form of energy unknown to our world yet.

Tesla devices...created by the team of Henry Ford, Thomas Edison, and Nicolas Tesla. Anything from lamps to frigs, to cooking devices. You name it; they've probably invented it in my world.

Moriarity...one of many. Professor Moriarity lives on in many and various manifestations for the sake of conflict, as well as invention and discourse. Where would a great detective be without a great villain to oppose him? While I don't feature Moriarity all the time, be warned he lurks behind the scenes! A lot!

Sherlock Holmes...A young man in his early twenties comes from a humble home and a good upbringing. Precocious with a perfect memory. Not the cold fish of the Doyle series. Much kinder and humorous. Still with many of the same characteristics, but softened with a gentler personality, without losing the edges that give him an engaging purpose and deductions that are utterly amazing at times.

Watson, Doctor John... the hero of the China Wars. Lost first love in China. Now in love with Mrs. Hudson. Loves Holmes like a brother. Doctor. Never without his black bag in which he carries his medical supplies and forensics tools that he and Sherlock often use in their investigations. Stocky with a bit of a stomach because of his love of scones, which I constantly use as a play of humor about the man.

Mrs. Hudson...not just a landlady anymore, but an integral part of the detective team...supplying support, as well as emotional and sometimes physical support. The glue that binds Watson and Holmes together. Again, in her twenties like Watson and Holmes. Lovely, but not beautiful, except in her beautiful spirit and kindly nature. Resourceful. Very shrewd and intelligent.

Lady Shareen...Lord Graystone's companion. A beautiful woman with a huge heart. She is responsible for helping women achieve social and financial equality. She also works to uplift the poor and homeless.

Professor Langston...the Invisible Man...a well-meaning doctor, who concocted a cocktail of chemicals that has forever altered his atomic structure such that he can turn invisible at will, though during emotional times of stress he can lose control of his visibility.

Inspector Bloodstone...a cantankerous policeman who has raving red hair, and a temper to match at times. Works with Holmes a lot but prefers to work on his own. Distrusts some of the intuitive moments of Holmes, but overall will go with what he reveals as Holmes is more often right than wrong in his deductions.

Constable Evans...the long-lost son of Inspector Bloodstone. Also red-haired, like his father, but with no temper and a great personality. Everyone likes him.

Queen Mary of Scots...has never existed. Instead, this one is a derivation of Mary, who was beheaded, and Victoria. Much more intelligent, progressive, but a leader in every sense of the word.

Magic...exists in this world of Sherlock as does science. Both are equally as relevant to the action and scenery of the stories.

Fairie...a land that exists in parallel to Sherlock's world and through which Lord Graystone (Lord of the Jungle) came through to become part of the Baker Street Brotherhood.

Fairie is richly endowed with magical creatures and monsters, Elves, fairies, and other fun things, as well as endless realms of green Amazon-like lands. Dragons. Which have played a part in several of my first stories and a few later ones.

Nicolas Tesla...a genius who has dedicated his life to upgrading the quality of life for everyone on the planet. Witty, charming, and dangerous.

Harry Houdini...swarthy, suave, into magic in every way...physical and the real thing.

Professor Challenger...very tall, built like a bear, flaming red beard and hair. Quick to temper, but a kind man with a great mind. An adventurer beyond measure.

Captain Nemo...a reformed pirate with a mind that grasps mechanics that rivals Henry Ford and Nicolas Tesla. Is famous for his extremely powerful weapon of the sea...the Nautilus.

Jules Verne...a genius when it comes to theories and fiction, blonde, extremely friendly, caring, and adventurous. Teams up often with H.G. Wells, a friend he grew up with. Designer of the Master of the World, which is another set of Victorian adventures he uses to fight an invasion from Mars.

H.G. Wells...a brilliant writer and navigator. Contributes to the flying device Master of the World and its ability to fly through space and time. Very British and a bit stuffy at times.

Alexander Dumas...a French friend of Jules in one of the worlds I've created for Jules to explore in unique adventures that do not include H.G. Wells. A huge man with a lust for adventure and fighting.

Henry Ford...still an arrogant man, but more willing to help others, and often teams up with Tesla to do projects. Not prominent yet in my stories but working on it.

Master of the World...a huge flying machine that resembles a cross between a dirigible and a submarine that travels utilizing String theory, with an engine that converts string energy into fuel that can thrust the ship between parallel worlds, as well as back and forth in time. Created by Jules Verne, but later improved by H.G. Wells after their battle with the Martians detailed in my prior series starting with Invaders.

Lord Graystone...my version of Tarzan, but instead of being raised by apes, he was raised by a bull dragon. Highly educated and a loyal supporter of Queen Mary of Scots and husband of Lady Shareen. Sponsors numerous charities for the poor and unwanted. Champion of Fairie.

Hyde...Doctor Jekyll performs an experiment on himself that separates the evil portion of him into a unique entity. This entity is pure evil and pure energy. It can possess anyone and once having done so, become that person. Cause them to do the unthinkable to achieve its evil plans.

Doctor Jekyll...a kind, young teacher who has made a horrible miscalculation and created an abomination of himself.... Hyde! A creature that is pure evil.

Dracula...not the Bran Stoker version, but my own. Misunderstood, not eternal, and drinking human blood when no other choice is possible.

Conan Doyle...the dead Sir Arthur Conan Doyle brought from our world to the alternate reality which he is reborn into, healthy and young once more. Also, an integral part of the great detective's team at times.

Baker Street Brotherhood...a team of operatives who, upon occasion, help Sherlock and Watson in their missions. Some of the more notable ones are Lord Graystone (Lord of the Jungle), Madame Curie, Dracula, Professor Langston (The Invisible Man), Professor Challenger (also a Conan Doyle character), Sir Arthur Conan Doyle himself (reborn from our world to the new one without losing awareness of himself), Lady Shareen (our equivalent of Indiana Jones), Jules Verne and H.G. Wells.

Monk...a spiritual leader and teacher, who has an ashram and school at the foot of the Himalayas in Pahalgam and is considered enlightened.

Also, the first and only teacher that Holmes felt truly affectionate for and close to.

There are many, many more, but these are the most frequently guested characters in my stories and novels.

Request for Review

If you found some pleasure in reading my work, please take the time to leave a review for it. Authors can thrive or die for the lack of reviews.

Thanking you in advance for your kindness.

John

Author's Note

Join my Baker Street Universes group to get things I don't usually share with others, and to hash over the universe I've created with me and fellow authors and readers.

My Baker Street Universes Facebook group is a place to interact with me frequently.